D0397099

HANDS OFF!

OFF!

PRIVATE

DIARY!

Fingerprint detector
working now!

←

Unfavorite Disasters—
the Worst of the Worst!

Daily Disaster Wednesday

1. A kid who really bugs you is standing next to your best friend.
2. You wave so your friend will come over, away from the annoying kid.
3. Your friend waves back for _you_ to go to _her_.
4. You shake your head, forget it, no way.
5. She waves some more.
6. You shake your head some more.
7. Finally she comes over to you.
8. And you blurt out, "That's the jerk I told you about!"
9. Your friend smiles all fakey-fake and says, "You mean someone else!"
10. And then you notice the kid right behind her, glaring at you.
11. Steps 1-10 are how to make someone NOT like you.

Daphne's Diary
of
Daily Disasters

by Marissa Moss

The Fake Friend!

Simon & Schuster Books for Young Readers

New York   London   Toronto   Sydney   New Delhi

SIMON + SCHUSTER BOOKS FOR YOUNG READERS
An imprint of Simon + Schuster Children's Publishing Division
1230 Avenue of the Americas, New York, New York 10020

SIMON + SCHUSTER BOOKS FOR YOUNG READERS is a
trademark of Simon + Schuster, Inc.
For information about special discounts for bulk purchases,
please contact Simon + Schuster Special Sales
at 1-866-506-1949 or business@simonandschuster.com.
The Simon + Schuster Speakers Bureau can bring authors to
your live event. For more information or to book an event, contact the
Simon + Schuster Speakers Bureau at 1-866-248-3049 or
visit our website at www.simonspeakers.com.
Also available in a Simon + Schuster Books for Young Readers paperback edition
A Paula Wiseman Book
Book design by Daphne (with help from Tom Daly)
The text for this book is hand-lettered.
Manufactured in China
0412 SCP
2 4 6 8 10 9 7 5 3 1
CIP data for this book is available from the Library of Congress
ISBN 978-1-4424-4014-2 (hc)
ISBN 978-1-4424-4015-9 (pbk)
ISBN 978-1-4424-4016-6 (eBook)

This book is dedicated to
Lori Stahl,
a totally true-blue
friend.

Unfavorite Disasters—

the Worst of the Worst!

Daily Disaster, Friday

1. It's Friday and I want to have plans for the weekend, so I ask friend A over.
2. A can't come, so I ask friend B.
3. B's busy, so I ask friend C, even though I don't really like C.
4. C says yes, so great, now I have plans!
5. Except now A invites me to do something really cool—go to the Super Trampoline place.
6. Only I can't because I have plans already.
7. With C, who isn't even really a friend.
8. Happy weekend!

What's the worst friend disaster?

Forgetting someone's birthday?

Breaking something they love?

Sitting on their lunch by mistake.

DAY ONE:

How come when people say "Have a nice day," the person they say it to usually does, like it's so easy to have everything work out? Unless you're me.

When anyone says "Have a nice day" to me, I end up with my usual disasters. I have the worst luck ever! My luck is <u>so</u> terrible that if I bought a lottery ticket, here's what would happen:

Hmmm, I'd pick my lucky numbers except I don't have any.

So I'd do the opposite — I'd pick my UNlucky numbers.

13	39	31
↑	↑	↑
which everyone knows is bad luck.	Just because it looks unfriendly	Backward 13 is also bad luck.

Then, of course, I'd lose the lottery ticket since losing stuff is more bad luck.

Lottery ticket dropped in a mud puddle.

And that's when they'd call my numbers as the lucky winner. Except I'm not lucky or a winner.

   So I shouldn't be surprised that Imogen Hakim wants nothing to do with me. Why should she? Some of my bad luck might rub off on her.

   Who's Imogen? Is she super lucky? I don't know. All I know is that she's somehow perfect. She seems like she'd be a super nice friend, lucky or not.

   In fact, I bet if she became my friend, then my luck would finally change. I've got to make it happen.

   But how?

Imogen

She's sweet, smart, funny, nice...

... generous, kind, and good at math and spelling.

She makes her friends feel really special, super lucky. I want that!

Plus, she carries her lunch in a cute plaid bag.

She wears a stylish jean jacket. (I can't draw how great this jacket really is.)

She has a voice as soft as bunny fur. How does she do that?

Yeah, how?

In other words, she's totally amazing! In every possible way!

I already have a best friend, Kaylee, but why can't I have two best friends, or even three or four? Why can't I be that kind of popular girl?

Kaylee is great too. ↓

She's funny and nice, and the kind of friend you can count on. ↑

But as much as I like her, I still like Imogen. Maybe Kaylee does too and we both can be her friend. That would be easiest.
So I asked Kaylee.

That's what I suspected. Even if Kaylee doesn't care about being Imogen's friend herself, she cares about _me_ being her friend. It's one of those complicated friendship rules. Kaylee listed them for me so I won't make any mistakes. I don't want to take the chance of losing a friend to gain a friend. That would be terrible math, like $+1 = -1 = $ a big fat zero!

FRIENDSHIP

by Daphne

1. You can't EVER be friends with your friend's enemies. It's another math equation.

friend + hatred = friend's enemy = hatred + you

See how it all balances out?

2. You **have** to be friends — or at least friendly — with your friend's friends.

friend + like = friend's friend = like + you

Again, it all adds up.

R U L E S

and Kaylee

3. Any new friends have to be agreed on by the existing friends.

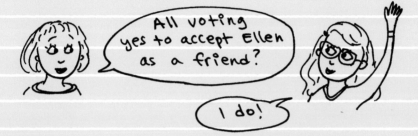

4. Any new enemies also have to be agreed on.

EXTRA

by Kaylee

And it gets more complicated...

1. A good friend allows you to have the first slice of pizza, the bigger piece of pie, the last french fry.

2. A good friend tells you if you have something gross stuck between your teeth or a booger hanging from your nose or eye gunk crusting up your eye.

RULES
and Daphne

3. A friend defends you if they hear anything bad about you.

That is so not true! She wasn't the one who farted in first period! She didn't fart until third period. I know! I was there!

4. A good friend never tells your secrets.

um, you know what I said about farting? Forget the whole thing. I was totally, completely wrong.

There were no farts of any kind.

POOOT!

Well, maybe one.

5. A good friend tells you which books are great, yes, read them, and which are terrible, forget about it.

6. A good friend can talk to you about movies without ruining the ending.

7. And they'll go to a movie twice so they can go with you.

And that's just the beginning of Kaylee's list! It's impressive all the things friends do. I wonder if I do all those things for Kaylee. I guess if I didn't, she wouldn't be my friend anymore, because she's the friendship expert.

Or maybe if I don't do them yet, she can tell I will someday. I do tell her about good books and I definitely share cookies with her.

But for me, it's simple. I thought a friend was someone you like and they like you back. Shows what I know!

my basic friend equation.
↓

nice, fun to be with, listens to you, talks to you = friend

So I showed Kaylee my drawing and description of Imogen.

"Hmmm," Kaylee said. "It sounds like you like her more than me."

"Of course not! You're my best, best, BEST friend. And always will be. She's just another possible friend."

I didn't know there was anything TO figure out. I thought I'd eat lunch with Imogen, then ask her over — with Kaylee, naturally. That didn't seem complicated at all!

Except Kaylee said, "No way, you can't do that!"

"I'm not saying we should steal someone's lunch! You act like I'm suggesting a crime!"

No lunch swiping!
↓

But eating lunch is okay, right?

No sitting on lunches either!
↓

Turns out there are rules to even <u>making</u> friends! Life was so much simpler in kindergarten. Then you could play in the sandbox together and be instant friends. For a whole day!

Kaylee had to explain it all to me. There are some kids you can just go up to and be friendly with to become friends.

I'm one of those kids. Anyone who wants to eat lunch with me or walk home with me or invite me over, can just do it because here I am.

And there are other kids who have what Kaylee calls "guard dogs" or "gatekeeper" friends. Those are the kids you have to be friends with first if you're ever going to get near the person you really want to be friends with.

It's like these friends check you out first. And they're not really your friend, they're fake friends on the way to the real friend. Does that make sense?

Unfortunately, Imogen has one of those guard dog friends.
↓

See the resemblance?
↘

Darla Spinks ↗

And she's not at all someone I want to be friends with. She's snobby and snarky and is always saying mean things about people. And <u>to</u> them.

Why does Imogen have a friend like her? She's so opposite of Imogen. She's <u>Un</u>Imogen!

Does Darla have to be my fake friend before Imogen becomes a real friend?

According to Kaylee, yes. There's no other way. Which just goes to show the bad luck I have. Again.

Plus Darla wears weird socks and shoves to be first in any line — even a line for school photos! Who cares about that? →

She couldn't say no without sounding nasty, so she said yes. It was kind of awkward at first, but Kaylee really helped out.

And now there's the Darla Spinks kind. Do I really want to be even a fake friend with her?

Kaylee said we should at least try. To her, it's a kind of game. To me, it's super serious!

If I didn't have Kaylee with me, I would have just given up. But since we were doing it together, it wasn't as scary. I mean, she, Darla, wasn't as scary.

I used my sweetest, nicest voice.

And I didn't even squeak!

Hey, Darla! Can Kaylee and I eat lunch with you guys?

Darla looked suspicious, like I was trying to sell her a used hot dog with extra onions. Which I would never do.

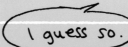
I guess so.

The kid who's so popular and powerful, you have to pretend to like them or your name is MUD.

Thanks for the invitation to your birthday party. I'm far too busy to come, but, of course, you <u>had</u> to invite me.

The worst part is, she's right!

The kid who <u>no one</u> likes, so you feel sorry for them and are extra nice to them, even though you don't like them either.

Wow! Nobody's ever invited me to a birthday party before.

I can't wait!

FAKE FRIENDS

What IS a fake friend? There are several kinds.

The kid you run into all the time because your moms shop at the same store, or you have the same doctor, but you don't really know them. Or like them.

Hi! So great to see you again!

The kid you don't particularly like, but you don't want to hurt their feelings, so you pretend to like them.

Meaning NEVER!

Some time real soon!

Yeah, you've got to come over some day.

That started a whole bunch of jokes about funny words and how you'll only use them on standardized tests. Imogen laughed! And so did Darla, amazingly enough. Is this the beginning of a fake friendship (with Darla) and a real one (with Imogen)?

Funny vocab words we <u>never</u> use:

Spotless — seen only in ads for dishwashing soap.

Or if your dog named Spot runs away. Then you're Spotless!

Twitch — now <u>that's</u> a handy word I use all the time, like "I was going to dress up as a twitch for Halloween."

↑ a twitchy witch

Delicatessen — everyone I know says "deli" — way easier to spell and quicker to say.

Deli means bagel store, basically.

I love lots of things about Imogen, like the way she thinks about math. She knows how to make math fun. She does these crazy math doodles, like when you see how many circles you can fit into a circle.

It all depends on how tiny you can draw. →

You can put circles in a triangle. ↶

Or even in a dog! Instead of spotless, mucho spots! ↰

↑

Believe it or not, this is doodling AND math because it's like you're drawing infinity.

It works with triangles, too. →

If my pen were tinier, I'd be drawing infinity triangles! ↰

She even showed me how to use circles to make a line of dogs that gets smaller and smaller, all in proportion. And it doesn't have to be dogs, it could be anything. Cats, mice, elephants, _anything_!

First draw two lines that meet.

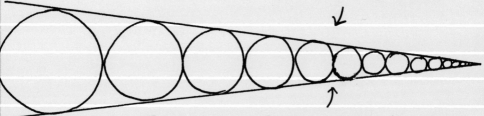

Then draw circles inside the lines.

Then add one dog (or cat or mouse) per circle.

It's easy!

This is Spot, the dog, again. He gets tiny pretty quickly, doesn't he?

While Imogen and I were doodling, Darla was glaring. I guess she doesn't like math. Or drawing. Or maybe me?

Math is boring no matter how much you doodle it. C'mon, Imogen, let's go.

But I like math. And I love doodling! Give me a second, Darla, and then we'll go.

She showed me one more doodle game, with a number spiral this time. That's the kind of thing you do for a friend, right?

After they left, I asked Kaylee what she thought.

"Imogen is nice enough. But that Darla! She's so sour!"

I wanted to say that sometimes sour is good, like in lemons or lemonade. Instead I said she wasn't _so_ bad. I wouldn't want her for a real friend, but for a fake one, she's fine.

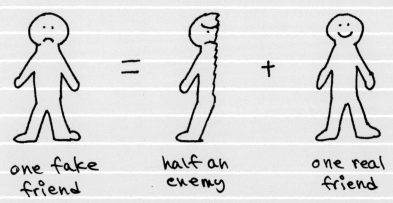

one fake friend = half an enemy + one real friend

My math is probably wrong here, but what I mean is, a fake friend is better than an enemy, not as good as a real friend, but totally okay if the fake friend leads to a _real_ friend.

Or one fake friend is less than an enemy, but also less than a real friend.

Kaylee said my equation didn't add up.
"Do you really want to be around Darla
just to be near Imogen? It's not worth
it to me. A fake friend isn't worth
anything as far as I'm concerned."

I think you're
annoyed by the idea
of fakeness. Think
of all the GOOD
fake things there
are.

fake fur →

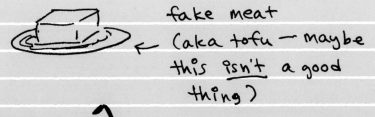
fake meat
(aka tofu — maybe
this isn't a good
thing)

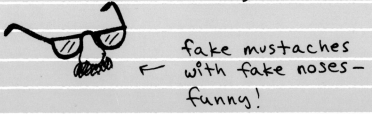
fake mustaches
with fake noses —
funny!

Tell you what — I'm such a real friend, I'll go along with you. Even though I'm not crazy about the idea.

We'll eat lunch with them again tomorrow and see if we can make some real friend progress.

Yay, Kaylee! She's the best, best friend, REAL best friend ever!

After school that day I wanted to make something for her so she'd know how much I appreciate her. ("Appreciate" is a vocab word, btw.)

I thought it'd be funny if I made her a fake present. I mean, it'd be a real present, but made from fake stuff. Kind of a joke present, something to make her laugh.

I wasn't sure what to make exactly, but I thought maybe I'd find some funny, fake ingredients in the twins' room, so that's where I looked first.

My little brothers are in kindergarten.
↓

↑
David has a perpetual booger bubbling from his nose, so that's how you know he's not Donald.

↑
Donald looks just like David, minus the booger.

I explained what I wanted and they said, okay, search all you want. Like it was perfectly normal for someone to ask for real fake stuff. Or fake real stuff. I told them I wanted both. Or either.

Here's what I found: possible ingredients for a funny fake present.

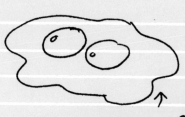

green plastic soldier

rubber eggs — both fake and somehow silly (better than rubber vomit or poop)

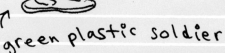

fuzzy dice — kinda fake because you can't really roll them.

tattoos — the fake kind that wash off

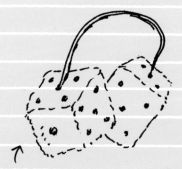

rubber witch fingers left over from Halloween — not really fingers, not really from a witch, so → twice the fakeness.

It seemed like I could make something good with all that, I just wasn't sure how. Or what.

Let me try!

No, me!

"You can both try," I said. "I don't have any ideas myself."
This is what they came up with:

Plastic soldier glued on top of a plain cardboard box.

? ? ? ? ? ? ?

MYSTERY

? BOX ?

Is what's inside real or only a dream? The fake soldier stands guard.

The twins told me what to write.

Once you opened the box, you saw the fuzzy dice on top of another box.

Not really dice, not really furry, fake both ways.

Again, I wrote what they suggested. I could see what they were doing and I figured out the rest myself.

Inside the dice box, I put another, smaller box with the rubber fingers taped on top. This time I wrote my own message on the side:

"Not-real fingers from a not-real witch— another double fake."

The next, smaller box had the toy eggs glued on top. →

Not really sunny-side up, not really eggs, but a good yolk!

Okay, it's a good joke, but a lame pun. ←

The last box had the tattoos inside.

And a message folded up on a piece of paper. This was the most important part of all— real words.

Real pictures, but fake tattoos to go with all the really fake stuff here. Just to show you how much fun fake things can be with a real friend like you!

I have to give my brothers credit. They helped me figure out the perfect way to prove how good fake stuff can be. Sometimes the twins really surprise me.

Thanks, you guys! This is so great.

I wouldn't have thought of this without you!

"Really?" asked Donald.

"Or fakely?" asked David.

"Both!" I said. "Really fakely and fakely really. You guys are geniuses!"

I just knew Kaylee would love it. It's her kind of creative, unusual present.

"Why all the fake stuff anyway?" David asked.

"It's complicated," I said. "You're too little to understand."

That was the exact wrong thing to say, and I knew it as soon as I'd said it, but it was too late. Now they'd both nag me forever until I answered them.

If the twins are _ever_ told they're too young or too little, they become GIANTS at stubbornness. As if they have to prove how old and big they are by becoming MAJOR pests!

So I explained the whole guard dog/ gatekeeper/ fake friend thing.

Donald thought the gatekeeper was like a soccer goalie making sure the ball stayed out.

David thought it was more like a loud, barking dog or the guard at the Emerald City in The Wizard of Oz.

Halt, who goes there?

Nobody gets to see the wizard.

In a way both of them were right. But the complicated bit, the part they couldn't understand, was the fake friend stuff.

"It's worth it to get past the guard, goalkeeper, fake friend person," I tried to explain. "Because then you get to the real friend who's <u>really</u> worth it."

"If you say so." David shrugged.

"If you do become friends with her — the fake one — in a fake way, I want to meet her," said Donald.

He'd be disappointed because he's imagining a fake friend like a robot.

Not a real person, but a real friend.

Darla is the opposite. She's a real person, but for me she'd be a fake friend. And not at all interesting to Donald or David.

Robot friends would be cool, I agree with them about that!

At school the next day, I tried to run up to Imogen first thing, but I was blocked — I mean really blocked — by Darla.

Daphne! If you have something to say to Imogen, you can tell me first!

Imogen didn't even seem to notice. She acted like this kind of thing was normal. Is it? It doesn't seem normal at all to me!

It's a free country," I said. "I can talk to whoever I want."

I knew I'd just made a bad, bad mistake. I was turning Darla into an enemy instead of a fake friend!

Why did I say that to her? Why did I have to be so dumb?

WHAT A DISASTER!!

I had to get back on her good side — if I'd ever <u>been</u> on her good side.

How, how, how, how, HOW, HOW??

I tried to think fast. And this is what I said.

"Me?" Darla arched one eyebrow. It's amazing how much one eyebrow arch can say. Her eyebrow was telling me she wasn't sure she could believe me.

So I laid it on thick.

yeah, I've been meaning to ask you where you got your shoes. They're super cute! I want a pair just like them.

Her shoes were kinda cute, not spectacular, but not boring. Would she believe me?

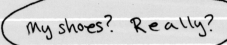

My shoes? Really?

There went her eyebrow again.

"Really, truly, really!" I said. "They look comfy AND cute. Plus, not too expensive so my mom might actually let me buy them."

I was totally rambling, blathering words before I could think about what I was saying.

And it worked!

yeah, they are great shoes. I got them at the store on Shattuck Avenue, the one by the movie theater.

↑ Relaxed, happy Darla face. No more suspicious eyebrow arching!

That started a whole clothes/shoe-shopping conversation where Darla did most of the talking and I just nodded my head and said "wow" and "cool" every now and then.

I felt like one of those bobblehead dogs people keep in their cars for some mysterious reason.

The bell rang and I had to go to class, so I never did get close to Imogen, but at least I fixed my big mistake with Darla. Disaster avoided!

It was like I put a bandage on a gigantic boo-boo!

The thing about making fake friends is that it's way more exhausting than making real friends. Why is lying and pretending so much worry and work?

At recess Kaylee asked if I still wanted to be friends with Imogen, and I had to admit I wasn't sure anymore.

It was a really hot summer and not only did this girl have a pool, she had all these fun floaty toys to play with.

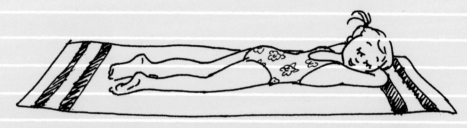

After we swam, we'd lie out in the sun and her mom would bring us lemonade and cookies. It was great!

Until the summer was over and it was too cold to swim, but Ellen still wanted to be friends.

Wanna come over today, Daphne? Or tomorrow? Or the next day?

But really I didn't want to be her friend. She smelled like tomato soup and being with her was like being with a cardboard box.

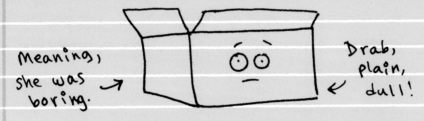

Meaning, she was boring. →

Drab, plain, ← dull!

I felt guilty and bad about myself and I promised myself I'd never do that again because it's not nice and I don't want to be that kind of person.

I wondered what Ellen was like now. She moved away last year and I was relieved because every time I saw her, I felt guilty.

When she left, I didn't have to feel guilty anymore.

Was Kaylee right? Was I doing the same kind of thing with Darla? Was I making a big, guilty mess for myself?

No, this was different. I wasn't trying to be friends with Darla. I was just throwing her a bone so she'd leave me alone and let me pass to get to Imogen. Kind of like bribing a guard dog or distracting it with a treat it can't resist. Was shoe admiration a kind of bone?

That made me think, maybe I was going about this the wrong way. Maybe I could just be honest with Darla and make a deal with her.

Darla, I want to be friends with Imogen, but not you. If I bring you a bag of candy or some cupcakes would you be okay with that?

If someone wanted to be friends with Kaylee, cupcakes would definitely sweeten the deal. Better than a bone or a doggy biscuit any day.

If I could just sit by Imogen, I could pass her notes and I wouldn't have to worry about Darla, but Ms. Underwood has us in assigned seats. I sit between Bruce and Lyndsey.

Bruce only cares about video games and sports.

Lyndsey is obsessed with her pet cat and sticker collection. I don't mean she collects pet cats — she has a cat.

Neither of them are friend material. We don't click at all.

Imogen is my kind of friend. Why doesn't she → know that?

She could try to be my friend instead of me trying to be hers. That would be so ← much easier!

Kaylee said she'd help me eat lunch with Imogen (and Darla) again. So we did, but this time Darla acted like she and I were already friends and Imogen was Kaylee's friend!

We could go shoe shopping together this weekend if you want. And maybe a movie.

That's really nice of you, but, um, I think we're visiting my grandparents. Maybe another time.

Did you read Bongo Fishing? That's a great book!

Really? Could you lend it to me?

HELP! I'm stuck with the wrong friend! The fake friend, not the real friend!

"What are you doing?" I hissed to Kaylee when the bell rang. "You're stealing my friend!"

"I am not! I don't want Darla for a friend. You can have her."

"Imogen! I mean Imogen! This isn't what was supposed to happen!"

Kaylee's my friend, but I hate it when she gets that smug I'm-right-you're-wrong-obviously look on her face. Especially when she IS right.

The moral of the story is you should be honest. I told you, fake friends are a BAD idea.

I was afraid to eat lunch with Imogen and Darla for the rest of the week. I didn't want Darla to get the wrong idea. But maybe I could say yes to shopping with Darla if Imogen would come too.

Kaylee warned that would be dangerous, like a ticking time bomb waiting → to blow up in your face.

Is she right? Am I making a terrible problem ← for myself?

If only I could figure out a way to be friends with Imogen WITHOUT Darla. Like, if Darla got sick and wasn't in school, that would give me my chance.
What if I tried the old poisoned pb&j trick? Of course, I wouldn't really poison her, but it's a thought.

yummy! →

Poison Butter ← and Jam

Kaylee came over this weekend and I gave her the fake present inside a fake present inside a fake present.
She loved it!

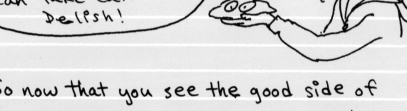

My favorite is the fake eggs, which I can fake eat. Delish!

"So now that you see the good side of fakeness, how do I make Darla a good fake friend?" I asked.

The same way I can make these fake eggs into a hat.

How do you like my egg hat?

I told Kaylee she was being silly. Fake eggs DON'T make a real hat.

"My point exactly," she said. "Fake friends can't be real anything, except a real pain. Just give up on this, Daphne. Lots of kids could be your friend. Why does it have to be Imogen?"

Because I'm stubborn. Like a mule. That's what my dad always says. When he's really mad at me he calls me Daphne Donkey. Which is slightly better than Donkey Daphne.

↑
Donkey or mule? Which one is it? How can you tell?

Still, I hate that! And a donkey isn't the same thing as a mule. Not that I want to be called Daphne Mule either.

Anyway, the point is I'm not giving up! I'll figure out a way no matter what.

The universe has answered my prayers!
Guess who stayed home from school today?

D A R L A !!

Which meant I could talk to Imogen all
I wanted. And she's just the kind of friend I
thought she'd be—funny and interesting and
nice.

She showed me more math doodles and games.
These are squiggle knots. Draw any loop that
ends where it begins. Now give it sides so
it has thickness like a rope. Now alternate
going over and under
each time the loop
meets itself.

The over-under parts will always alternate.
No matter how many twists and turns the loop
makes. Why? It's math magic!

I actually like division and fractions, too. I like how everything's neat and organized in math and the answers are all clear. There are no disasters in math! Unless you don't study.

Kaylee just puts up with my math mania. Imogen multiplies it exponentially — she's mathier than me!

So we had a great week together until day three, when Darla came back to school.

Then suddenly it was like Imogen didn't know who I was.

I waved frantically.

Hi, Imogen! Hi, Darla!

And they both ignored me. Totally.
I asked Kaylee what happened.
"I told you all this math stuff doesn't
add up. One Darla plus one Imogen equals
no friend for you."

I didn't get what she meant at all.
"Do I have to spell it out for you?" Kaylee
asked. "When **Darla's** around, Imogen drops
you. She was just being a temporary friend
because Darla was absent. I told you—if
you want Imogen for a friend, you have to
be friends with Darla first. Otherwise the
only kind of friend she'll be is a part-time
one. Temporary, like I said."

"A temporary friend?! What do you mean by that?"

"You know," Kaylee explained, "like when you're friends with someone you meet on vacation or in camp and you say you'll write and stay in touch and maybe you do for a little while, but soon you forget about each other completely."

Like the kid you spend hours with at the beach building a sand castle.

You don't even know each other's name but you have a great day together. When the tide comes in and washes your sand castle out to sea, your temporary friendship goes with it...

leaving nothing behind but sand.

"Ugh!" I said. "That's almost as bad as a fake friend."

"Well, maybe I'm wrong." Kaylee shrugged. "Maybe Imogen is still your friend, but she's so excited to see Darla again, she's distracted."

Kaylee could be right, but I had a new math doodle I really wanted to show Imogen. That seemed a great excuse to talk to her. I needed to know if she was a real friend or a temporary one.

So at lunch, I took my chance. Of course, I had to say something to Darla first.

Hey, Darla, glad you're feeling better.

Imogen, I have this amazing math doodle I just know you'll love.

Then before she could say anything,
I started to draw.
"Look," I said. "It's a new math doodle
and I got the idea from the over-under
loops you showed me. You start the same
way, with a big squiggle that ends where
it begins with all the loops nice and neat so
you can
see the
crossings.

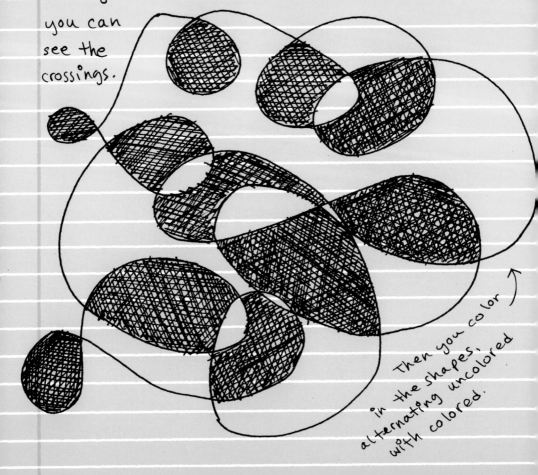

Then you color
in the shapes,
alternating uncolored
with colored.

"See how it works?" I asked. "No matter how random your squiggle or how many times the lines cross over, there will never be two colored parts next to each other. The pattern will always alternate. Cool, huh?"

I could tell from Imogen's eyes that she was interested, but she just nodded and smiled.

"Thanks for the show-and-tell," Darla said. "It's a great demonstration of how some things don't mix. If you know what I mean."

"Yeah," I said. "You can do the same thing with a bunch of different shapes, that overlap, not just a squiggle. See?"

Even when you think it won't work, it always does.

"And I can do the same thing with you!" Darla said. "Meaning you don't mix well with me, get it? Go your separate way— far, far away!"

"But I thought we were friends. We were going to go shopping and everything," I babbled. I seem to babble a lot with Darla.

"Except you didn't want to! I was nice to you and you avoided me! Not very friendly, if you ask me!"

She looked furious and, honestly, when she said it that way, I couldn't blame her.

I messed up. I really, truly did.

That's NOT a true friend!

"Of course she was!" Darla snapped. "She's not a friend— she's a friend stealer! She's trying to steal you away from me! What kind of friend is that?"

Was that me? Was that really what I was doing?

I had thought Darla was the fake friend all this time. What if I was? That would be horrible!

So I took a deep breath and did the hardest thing I've ever done.

I said I was sorry.

I didn't mean to be like that and I'm really, truly sorry because I never meant to be a friend thief.

I tried to explain it the best I could. "I just like talking to Imogen about math doodles and I know you don't like that kind of stuff, Darla, so I thought we weren't really friends."

I wanted to be nice, but there was no way to explain the shoe-shopping mistake. The last thing I could do was tell the truth.

Then Kaylee, my 100% true friend, came to my rescue.

"Don't mind Daphne," she said. "She's a total disaster when it comes to figuring out friends, friendship, fake friends, and real friends. You have to admit that can be tough and confusing sometimes. But the important thing is, she's not mean. She may make mistakes. She might hurt your feelings. But not on purpose. She's too nice for that.

"And she's definitely NOT a friend stealer. No way, no how."

Thank you, Kaylee!

You're the best friend ever!

Darla grunted. But she looked less mad.

"Can I try again?" I asked. "Why don't both of you—no, all of you—Kaylee, Darla, and Imogen come over to my house tomorrow?"

"Really?" Darla asked. "This isn't a trick?"

"No trick!" I promised. And it wasn't. I mean, was Darla really that bad? If Imogen likes her, can't I? Maybe we could all be friends?

↑
It's another kind of math doodle, a chain of paper dolls all connected.

After school I asked Kaylee what she thought. Could she like Darla and Imogen? Would she be willing to at least try?

"Dunno," said Kaylee. "We'll see what happens tomorrow, but I think having more friends is a good thing. So long as I'm still your best friend."

"Are you kidding? You saved my life today!"

Super-Kaylee ↑ to the rescue!

I told David and Donald that I was having friends over tomorrow so they better behave and stay out of our hair.

"Real friends or fake friends?" Donald asked.

"The kind that's like plastic toy eggs?" asked David.

"Real friends," I said. And I meant it.

No more fake friends for me! Either I really like Darla or I don't, but I'm going to really, truly give her a chance.

"So no plastic egg friends? Too bad! I was curious to see what they were like," said David.

"I wanted robot friends myself," Donald added.

Disappointing for them, I guess.

At dinner Mom and Dad were talking about boring grown-up stuff and I wasn't really listening until Mom said something I couldn't ignore.

"All these fake friends are driving me crazy with their messages about what they're doing and eating and wearing and reading. Who cares? Why write about all that petty stuff?"

"Fake friends?" I interrupted. "Grown-ups have fake friends? I thought that was a kid thing."

"Mom's talking about friends on the Internet," Dad explained. "People you might not know or maybe you met them once a long time ago, but now they want to be your friend."

"Be your friend how?" I asked. "Like, do stuff with you?"

"No!" snapped Mom. "That's the fake part. They don't even really want to know you. They just want to say they do, so it'll look like they're popular, like they have more friends than they really do. As if somebody is keeping score!"

Robot friends are better than that!

Or invisible, pretend friends!

I agree with my brothers! Kids have realer fake friends than grown-ups do. Who'd have guessed?

Now I don't feel so bad about my Darla disaster. At least I'm really having her over, we'll really do something together, and who knows, maybe we'll really be friends.

And no matter what, I have a real friend in Kaylee.

I thought we'd make cookies, but something totally amazing happened when Darlee, Imogen, and Kaylee all came over.

All because I was nervous.

I'm so glad to have all of you here!

I never, ever wanted to be a friend stealer!

I want us all to be real, true good friends.

"Is there any other kind?" Darla asked, arching that famous eyebrow of hers.

Kaylee elbowed me, but it was too late — I'd already said too much. My mouth should be declared a disaster zone! I never say anything right!

David and Donald ran in just then and
I knew they'd say something that would
get me into even deeper trouble.
So I decided to say it myself first.
"I meant, no fake friends, people who
aren't really your friends, but say they are
or people you don't really like, but you
pretend to be friends with. My mom was
just talking about that last night. Did
you know grown-ups have fake friends?"

There was an awkward silence and for a
second I thought Darla would stomp out
with Imogen right behind her.
But she didn't.
She laughed. Really, truly, from deep
in the belly laughed!

"I know just what you mean!" she said when she finally caught her breath. "You should hear my mom talk about her so-called friends!"

That broke the ice and everyone was telling fake friend stories. Until Darla had a brilliant idea. Instead of math doodles, she suggested we make a friend chart.

> See, I do like to doodle, but people are way more interesting to draw than spirals or loops.

I still like math doodles, but I had to agree with her.

Here's what we made:
(well, not <u>here</u> – on the next page.)

FRIEND

How close are you?

Best friends—people you like most and spend the most time with.

Close friends—people you tell your secrets to.

Friends—people you like and spend time with.

Sort of friends—people you don't know well, but you do know their names.

CHART

What kind of friend?

Know-names — people you don't know well, but you do know their names.
You don't like them, but you don't dislike them either.

Acquaintances — people you've seen before even if you can't remember where.

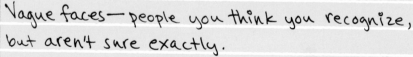

Vague faces — people you think you recognize, but aren't sure exactly.
And don't really care.

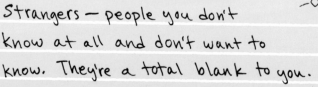

Strangers — people you don't know at all and don't want to know. They're a total blank to you.

We didn't end up making cookies, but we did make friends, nothing fake about it. Once I got to know Darla, I actually liked her. She's funny—in a sharp way—but still funny.

Who knew a fake friend could become a real one? And that a disaster could be a great opportunity!

Maybe my luck is changing after all, and it's time to buy a school raffle ticket. I could win the grand prize—a trip to Adventureland with a friend.

I'd ask Kaylee, the best friend in the world. It's always an adventure with her— not the disastrous kind. That's a real friend for you!

Friends — fake OR real — don't read friends' diaries!

SO NO SNOOPING!

Friend Disasters

Wrong reasons to pick a friend:

Because they can help you with your homework.

Because you like their dog.

Because they have an amazing house— who cares about them?

Because everyone else wants to be their friend, so you feel left out.

Because they have a great comic collection. ↗

↑
Because their brothers are super cute.

Because they'll trade lunches with you.

Because next to them, you look tall.

Because they hate chocolate or anything sweet. And you don't.

Because they really, really like you, even though you don't like them.

Kaylee, have you ever had a fake friend?

Don't you remember that girl in second grade? The one I _thought_ really liked me?

Didn't she? She went over to your house a lot.

Yeah, but not for me! She liked the kind of salami my mom bought for snacks. She came to visit my refrigerator, not me!

Hey, I like that salami too.
That's not such a bad reason
for friendship.

DAPHNE!!

I'm kidding! Can't
a friend joke with you?

Okay, but next time
you come over, NO
salami for you!

Any bologna
then?

What's the worst thing you can say
to someone you want to be your friend?

um, I forgot
your name. What
is it?

That wasn't
me who farted.

Wow, you're so tall!
How's the weather
up there?

Wow, you're
so short! Do you
get stepped on by
mistake?